LAURENCE KING

PUBLISHED IN 2018 by
LAURENCE KING PUBLISHING LTD.
361-373 CITY ROAD
LONDON EC1V 1LR
TEL: + 44 20 7841 6900
FAX: + 44 20 7841 6910
www.laurenceking.com
enquiries @ laurenceking.com

A CATALOGUE RECORD OF THIS BOOK IS
AVAILABLE FROM THE BRITISH LIBRARY.

ISBN 978-1-78627 0696

Printed in China.

THANKS TO:
LAURENCE KING
DONALD DINWIDDIE
ELIZABETH JENNER
FELICITY AWDRY
NATASCHA BIEBOW
VANESSA GREEN
ELIZABETH SHEINKMAN
ANGUS HYLAND
Harriet & Alexander

For
Jake

Bob's
Blue Period

Written and Illustrated by
Marion Deuchars

LAURENCE KING

Bob and Bat are best friends.

They do EVERYTHING together....

Best of all, they love painting.

But one day, Bob couldn't find Bat anywhere, only a note.

Bob felt lost without his best friend.

"Maybe I'll do some painting," said Bob.

So, he painted a banana—
a BLUE banana.

He painted an orange—
a **BLUE** orange.

He painted a tree—
a **BLUE** tree.

In fact, everything he painted,
he painted BLUE.

THERE was a **BIG BLUE HOLE**
where BAT used to be.

Owl and Cat came to have their portraits painted.

"WHERE'S BAT? and what happened to ALL the COLOURS" whispered the birds.

"BBBRRR" shuddered Owl.

2

CAT put ON his NEW hat and TIE. "I'm ready" he said nervously.

So Bob painted Cat.

"OH DEAR, I guess it's my turn!" said Owl.

So Bob painted Owl.

Bob missed Bat
so much that his
whole world was
turning BLUE!

"WHAT to Do?"
hooted Owl.

"WE HAVE GOT TO DO SOMETHING!"
shouted the birds.

They had an IDEA.

"Bob!
there is
something you have
GOT to SEE!"
And grabbing him,
they ran for the door.

Out into the night they went.

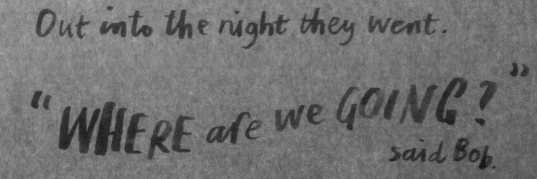

" WHERE are we GOING ?"
said Bob.

Out into the night they went.

"ARE WE there YET?" pleaded Bob.

They reached the top of the hill just as
the sun was rising.

"WOW!
WHo PAINTED that!"

He'd forgotten how many beautiful colours there are in the world.

Excited but very tired, Bob went home to sleep.

His dreams were full of COLOUR.

When Bob woke up
he felt so DIFFERENT.

Just then, a postcard dropped through the letterbox.

"Bat is coming home!"
cried Bob

Dear Bob
I've had a very long sleep in a lovely damp, dark cave. I really missed you, but now I feel better and I'm on my way home.
Your best friend
Bat x

Bob the Artist
2 Berry Lane
Great Britain
SG1 A0B

And he opened the door and there was Bat....
"Did you get my card?" asked Bat.

All the friends had a BIG PARTY to celebrate Bat's return.

Now Bob's world is FULL of COLOUR again.

He paints his grass GREEN,
his oranges ORANGE and
his bananas...